TOOLS FOR CAREGIVERS

- **F&P LEVEL:** C
- **WORD COUNT:** 42

- **CURRICULUM CONNECTIONS:** community, community helpers

Skills to Teach

- **HIGH-FREQUENCY WORDS:** a, am, do, get, he, how, I, is, much, my, she, they, this
- **CONTENT WORDS:** checkups, checks, doctor, ears, eyes, heart, nice, shot, sticker, tall, weigh
- **PUNCTUATION:** exclamation points, periods
- **WORD STUDY:** compound word (*checkups*); /k/, spelled *c* (*doctor*); /k/, spelled *ck* (*checkups, checks*); long /a/, spelled *ei* (*weigh*); long /e/, spelled *ea* (*ears*); r-controlled vowels (*heart*)
- **TEXT TYPE:** factual description

Before Reading Activities

- Read the title and give a simple statement of the main idea.
- Have students "walk" though the book and talk about what they see in the pictures.
- Introduce new vocabulary by having students predict the first letter and locate the word in the text.
- Discuss any unfamiliar concepts that are in the text.

After Reading Activities

Doctors are community helpers. They work in our communities and help keep us healthy. Ask students to name other community helpers. List them on the board. Would the students like to be any of these community helpers when they grow up? Which would they like to be, and why?

Tadpole Books are published by Jump!, 5357 Penn Avenue South, Minneapolis, MN 55419, www.jumplibrary.com

Copyright ©2021 Jump. International copyright reserved in all countries. No part of this book may be reproduced in any form without written permission from the publisher.

Editor: Jenna Gleisner **Designer:** Michelle Sonnek

Photo Credits: Africa Studio/Shutterstock, cover (clipboard and stethoscope); Mega Pixel/Shutterstock, cover (reflex hammer); New Africa /Shutterstock, cover (tongue depressor); Alexander Raths/Shutterstock, 1; Karl_Sonnenberg/Shutterstock, 2tr, 3 (background); wong yu liang/ Shutterstock, 2tr, 3 (foreground); FatCamera/iStock, 2bl, 4–5; Science Photo Library/SuperStock, 2br, 6–7; Photographee.eu/Shutterstock, 8; Serhii Bobyk/Shutterstock, 9; SofikoS/Shutterstock, 2tl, 10–11; fstop123/iStock, 2ml, 12–13; 5 second Studio/Shutterstock, 2mr, 14–15; wavebreakmedia/Shutterstock, 16.

Library of Congress Cataloging-in-Publication Data
Names: Zimmerman, Adeline J., author.
Title: Doctor's office / by Adeline J. Zimmerman.
Description: Minneapolis, MN: Jump!, (2021) | Series: Around town | Includes index. | Audience: Ages: 3–6
Identifiers: LCCN 2019047610 (print) | LCCN 2019047611 (ebook) | ISBN 9781645274681 (hardcover) | ISBN 9781645274698 (paperback) | ISBN 9781645274704 (ebook)
Subjects: LCSH: Children—Medical examinations—Juvenile literature. | Medical offices—Juvenile literature. | Physicians—Juvenile literature.
Classification: LCC RJ50.5 Z56 2021 (print) | LCC RJ50.5 (ebook) | DDC 610.69—dc23
LC record available at https://lccn.loc.gov/2019047610
LC ebook record available at https://lccn.loc.gov/2019047611

DOCTOR'S OFFICE

by Adeline J. Zimmerman

TABLE OF CONTENTS

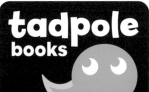

WORDS TO KNOW

checkups

doctor

shot

sticker

tall

weigh

DOCTOR'S OFFICE

doctor

This is a doctor!

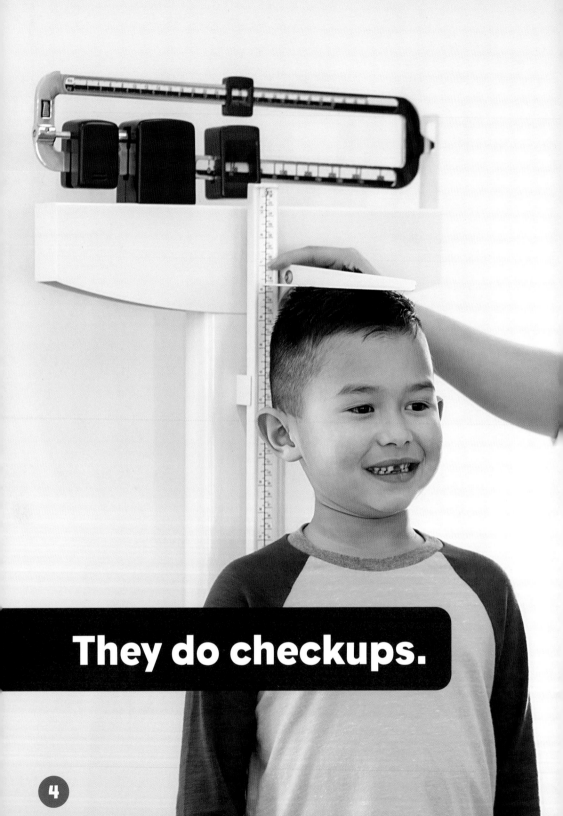

They do checkups.

She checks how tall I am.

scale

She checks how much I weigh.

He checks my ears.

He checks my eyes.

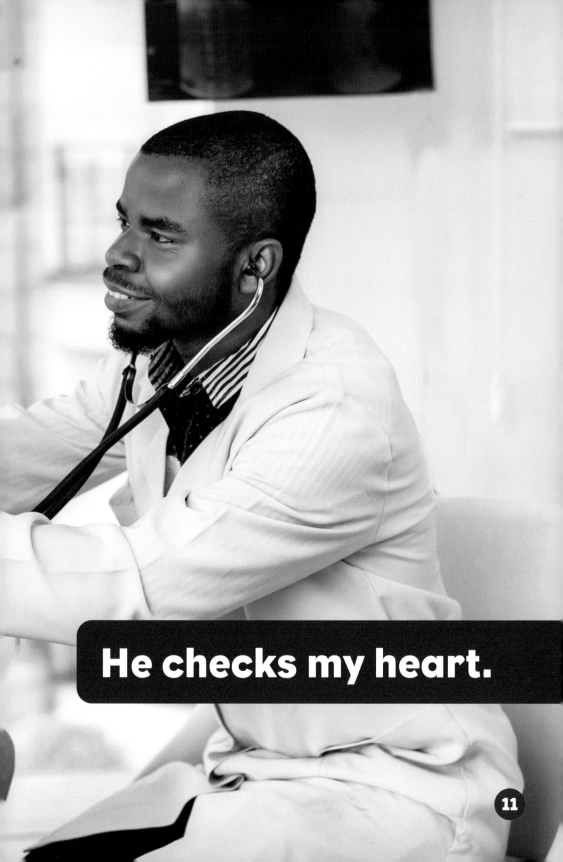

He checks my heart.

shot

I get a shot.

I get a sticker!

Nice!

LET'S REVIEW!

What is this doctor checking?

INDEX